BIONICLE™

CHRONICLES #2

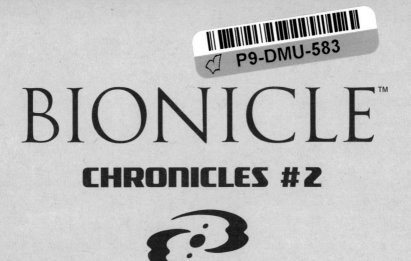

Beware the Bohrok

by C.A. Hapka

SCHOLASTIC INC.
New York Toronto London Auckland Sydney
Mexico City New Delhi Hong Kong Buenos Aires

ISBN 0-439-50117-2

Design by Peter Koblish

24 23 22 21 20 19 18 17 16 15 14   6 7 8/0

Printed in the U.S.A.
First printing, August 2003

The Legend of Mata Nui

In the time before time, the Great Spirit descended from the heavens, carrying we, the ones called the Matoran, to this island paradise. We were separate and without purpose, so the Great Spirit blessed us with three virtues: unity, duty, and destiny. We embraced these gifts and, in gratitude, we named our island home Mata Nui, after the Great Spirit himself.

But our happiness was not to last. Mata Nui's brother, Makuta, was jealous of these honors and betrayed him. Makuta cast a spell over Mata Nui, who fell into a deep slumber. Makuta's power dominated the land, as fields withered away, sunlight grew cold, and ancient values were forgotten.

Still, all hope was not lost. Legends told of six mighty heroes, the Toa, who would arrive to save Mata Nui. Time would reveal that these were not simply myths — for the Toa did appear on the shores of the island. They arrived with no memory, no knowledge of one another — but they pledged to defend Mata Nui and its people against the darkness. Tahu, Toa of Fire. Onua, Toa of Earth. Gali, Toa of Water. Lewa, Toa of Air. Pohatu, Toa of Stone. And Kopaka, Toa of Ice. Great warriors with great power, drawn from the very elements themselves. Together, they were six heroes with one destiny: to defeat Makuta and save Mata Nui.

This is their story.

UNDERGROUND

Clean it all . . . it must be cleaned.

The creature stirred and opened its eyes.

Clean it all . . . clean it all. . . .

It felt confusion. It wanted, needed to move. To clean.

It must be cleaned it must be cleaned it must be cleaned. . . .

The creature pushed against the hard, silent objects surrounding it in the darkness. One of the objects shifted.

Clean it all, the second being's mind offered sleepily.

It must be cleaned, the first agreed, strangely relieved. *It must be cleaned.*

All obstacles will be removed.

It must be cleaned. It will be cleaned.

The first creature's panic faded. It was not time yet. The time would come — soon. But not yet.

It relaxed and fell silent again. All was dark and still.

For now.

THE CALM BEFORE
THE STORM

The Toa couldn't contain their joy. Finally! Out of the darkness of the tunnels, safe from Makuta and his minions, free to enjoy the sunlight and the beauty of the island. Except . . .

"I wonder what Makuta has in store for us next," Gali, Toa of Water, said, and a shadow settled over the group.

Tahu, Toa of Fire, nodded. None of them knew much about the dark being known as Makuta. The six Toa had arrived on Mata Nui remembering nothing but their names and a few snippets of confusing and frightening dreams. But they soon learned of their duty — to protect the island and its people from the powers of darkness.

The Fire Toa touched his mask, feeling the energy humming beneath its golden surface. Each Toa wore a golden Kanohi mask just like his. The masks' awesome powers had just helped the Toa defeat the fearsome Rahi.

"I bet Makuta is deephiding now that he's seen our fightpower," Lewa, Toa of Air, said, puffing out his green chest proudly. "He won't soon fearchallenge Mata Nui again."

"Such bragging seems unwise and unnecessary," said Kopaka, Toa of Ice, in a cold voice.

Onua, Toa of Earth, was about to agree — in a gentler way — when he sensed the ground tremble beneath him. "Quiet," he ordered abruptly, raising a hand to the other Toa.

Tahu, Lewa, and Gali paused and glanced at him. "What is it?" Lewa asked eagerly. "Do you feel something? Hear something? Is it Mata Nui awakening, do you think?" The Toa had never forgotten their ultimate goal: to awaken the spirit of Mata Nui. Now that Makuta's Rahi had been vanquished, there seemed to be nothing standing in their way.

"I don't know." Onua frowned, focusing his mind on the earth below him. Now it came again — a shudder, as if the entire island were shifting in its sleep. Was it Mata Nui emerging?

The next tremble was stronger. "Whoa!" Gali shouted. "Brothers, if this *is* Mata Nui, I fear he's in a very bad mood!"

The earth shuddered again, with a grinding of stone against stone and the creak and roar of falling trees and tumbling rocks. Onua braced himself against a nearby swell and closed his eyes as yet another spasm shook the land. Could this be Mata Nui? Or had they awakened someone — or something — else?

THE AWAKENING

The creature, deep in slumber, felt the trembling of the earth.

It awoke. This time, there was no mistake.

It is time.

As the thunderous vibrations rocked the cave, another creature stirred, and another. Dozens upon hundreds upon thousands.

They shook off their long, deep sleep. Energy poured through them, along with absolute knowledge. Their duty waited. It was time.

It must be cleaned. It is time. Clean it all.

It is time. All obstacles will be removed.

Clean it all. It must be cleaned.

It is time.

*　　*　　*

"Look!" Pohatu, Toa of Stone, shouted, pointing at a figure revealed by the falling trees. "It's one of Tahu's villagers!"

Tahu leaped forward, surprised to find anyone from his fiery village of Ta-Koro so far from home. The Matoran was lying on the ground, his legs trapped by a fallen tree branch. He seemed stunned, and was muttering one word over and over.

Quickly freeing the villager, Tahu leaned closer, trying to hear him. "Speak," he said. "What brings you so far from Ta-Koro?"

The villager was still babbling, not making any sense.

"What's he saying?" Gali asked.

The Matoran seemed unaware of the Toa's presence. He stared blindly ahead, his eyes cloudy with terror.

"*Bohrokbohrokbohrokbohrok*," he muttered tonelessly.

"What?" Pohatu stepped closer, looking confused. "What is it? What's he saying?"

"Little brother!" Lewa said loudly, touching the Matoran on the shoulder. "What is it? What's wrong? We're here to help you."

The Matoran didn't react. He hardly seemed to pause for breath as he babbled on in the same rapid, frightened voice. "*Bohrokbohrokbohrokbohrok . . .*"

"What's he saying?" Pohatu repeated.

"One word, over and over," Tahu reported. "*Bohrok.* I must return to Ta-Koro immediately."

"We'll go, Tahu," Gali spoke up.

Onua nodded. "If there is a threat to your village, it is a threat to all our people."

Tahu accepted with a quick bow of his head. Then, slinging the Matoran over his shoulder, he gestured for the others to follow.

He raced through the trees and meadows toward the foothills of the Mangai. The others were close behind him.

"I have just one question," Pohatu said after a few minutes. The Toa had quickly crossed the flatlands and foothills and were now climbing steadily toward the village perched near the topmost slopes of the mountain.

"What's that?" Gali asked.

"What's a Bohrok?" Pohatu wondered.

Tahu, who was still in the lead, skidded to a halt. He stood on a ledge overlooking the village of Ta-Koro.

"I fear we have just found out."

THE ARRIVAL

The Toa gaped in amazement at the sight before them. In the distance, Ta-Koro rose against the rocky slope of the mountain, its stone gates and magma buildings unharmed. But the plain before it was in ruins.

Thick black smoke poured from piles of rubble and gouges in the earth. Trees and plants had been ripped out by the roots and tossed about like toys. Near the gates, frightened villagers milled around, shouting and crying with panic.

"What could have caused this?" Lewa whispered to Gali worriedly.

Gali pointed. "Them. Look!"

Dozens of strange creatures were moving across the plain — large two-legged armored beasts with powerful-looking claws. Some were silvery-white and some bronze, and a few were much smaller than the others, but all scuttled about like enormous insects. As Lewa watched, several of the bronze beasts gathered together, then stormed straight into a small hill, leveling it to the ground.

Tahu set the still-stunned Matoran on the ground. "Stay here," he said firmly, hoping the villager understood. "We'll deal with this!"

The others were already rushing forward to stop the strange creatures. Lewa reached one of the bronze-colored ones just as it headed toward a small clump of trees. "Let's see how these things stand up to a cyclone!"

He leaped into the air in front of the creature and breathed in, preparing to summon the winds to his aid. But before so much as a breeze had stirred, the creature moved forward, letting out an unearthly screech.

Lewa reeled as an icy blast of cold air struck him. "What? Ice?" he cried, struggling to remain in the air. But it was no use. He was frozen in a block of ice, unable to move or even levitate. He crashed to the ground with a thud.

"Away from him, creatures!" Tahu cried, leaping forward and dragging Lewa out of harm's way.

Lewa shook off the ice, which melted quickly near Tahu's sword. He jumped to his feet, ready to face the creature again.

But the creature showed no interest in him. Instead it uprooted a tree and then moved on toward a large lava hill.

"This is crazy," Onua called from somewhere nearby. "They aren't harming the villagers; they ignore us unless we get right in their way! So why all this chaos?"

"I don't know," Pohatu said. "But we have to stop them!"

Everywhere Lewa looked he saw more of the strange creatures. "But how?" he exclaimed. "There are so many of them!"

Tahu knew they had to do something fast if there was any hope of saving his village. Suddenly he had an idea.

"Lewa!" he cried. "Gali! Combine your powers!"

Raising their arms, Lewa and Gali summoned the winds and the rain. Soon a mighty storm raged above the peak.

KA-BOOOOOOM!

An enormous blast of lightning rocked the valley in front of the village. The destructive beasts were tossed high into the air, sparking and shrieking. As they landed, they scuttled for shelter. Soon all had disappeared.

All but one. It lay damaged and stunned, legs waving weakly in the air.

"They're gone for now," Pohatu commented, bending over the injured creature. "They left us a prisoner, too. But what's in its head?"

The others gathered around for a better look at their new enemy. The sloping shield that covered its head had been thrown back by the impact. A glowing, green object lay inside.

Before they could figure out what it might be, a voice spoke from behind them. "I know the answers you seek, though I wish I did not."

It was the leader of the villagers of Ta-Koro. "Turaga Vakama!" Pohatu said. "What is it? What are these creatures?"

The Turaga sighed. "We have known the legends of the Bohrok for centuries, and we prayed they were only legends. But the Bohrok are real — all too real. And they are swarming over all of Mata Nui."

"Tell us more," Tahu ordered, stepping forward to face his village's Turaga. "We need to know what we face."

Vakama nodded. "It is said the Bohrok sleep an eternal sleep, waiting to hatch. Once awakened, the swarms are unstoppable — a force so powerful, they can reduce mountains to rubble and turn rivers dry as the desert sands. These creatures do not work alone."

"Right," Pohatu said. "They have those smaller creatures with them — like little scouts or something."

"Those are the Bohrok Va," Vakama said. "And you are right — they are smaller, quicker creatures that act as scouts and couriers. But that's not what I meant. You see, each Bohrok carries within it a krana."

"That?" Kopaka asked, pointing to the glowing object inside the disabled Bohrok. "Is that the krana?"

"It looks like a mask," Pohatu observed.

"Yes," Vakama said. "It gives them purpose and power. Their krana are their greatest strength — but also their greatest weakness. Even the mightiest of Bohrok can be humbled if parted from its krana."

"These krana," Tahu said. "Do they come from Makuta?"

Vakama shook his head. "That we do not know," he said. "The legends do not offer an answer."

The Toa listened carefully as the Turaga outlined the different swarms of Bohrok. Those like the one that had blasted him with its icy breath were known as the Kohrak. The bronze-colored ones were the Pahrak, which could turn mountains to crumbling stone. The stealthy Gahlok hid beneath the waves and struck when least expected. The fiery Tahnok were capable of melting through any substance, while the powerful Nuhvok lurked below the surface and dug mazes of tunnels to weaken the structures that stood above. Most feared of all were the Lehvak, whose acid venom could dissolve even solid rock.

"All right," Lewa said when the Turaga paused for breath. "Enough of the feartalking. What do we do to defeat these Bohrok?"

"Now that the swarms have awakened, only one hope remains," Vakama said. "You must collect the eight breeds of krana from each Bohrok swarm. They will unlock the secret to the Bohrok's defeat."

"Eight breeds of krana?" Gali asked. "What do you mean?"

"Like the Bohrok themselves, the krana serve different purposes," Vakama explained. "Each type looks slightly different. The one you see there is one of the Krana Xa, the swarm commander." He pointed to the disabled Bohrok again. "You must gather one of each type of krana from each of the six swarms."

"But why?" Pohatu asked. "What will that tell us?"

"The knowing will come," Vakama replied. "That is all that has been foretold."

Tahu grimaced. *The knowing will come.* The Toa had been hearing that phrase since arriving on the island.

He grabbed the krana inside the fallen Bohrok. It was warm and squishy, slightly heavier than it looked. He stared at it, wondering how something so small could cause so much damage and devastation. "Return to your villages," he told the others. "If gathering these krana will save Mata Nui, then that's what we'll do."

"What do you mean?" Gali said. "We can't split up now — not when a new danger threatens Mata Nui. Didn't we learn anything from the fight against the Rahi? We are much more powerful when we're all together. Unity —"

"— Duty, destiny," Tahu said impatiently, finishing the common Matoran saying. "Yes, I know. But if these things are all over Mata Nui, we need to meet them wherever they are."

"Tahu is right," Kopaka said. "My village needs me. I must go there."

Gali was so surprised to hear Kopaka agreeing with Tahu that she couldn't speak for a moment. "All right," she said at last. "Perhaps we should see to our own villages. But be careful. And let's plan to meet again soon."

As the others nodded, Vakama held up his hand. "A warning before you go, brave Toa," he said urgently. "Beware the krana! When worn, they can steal the mind — and even the Toa might not be able to resist such terrible power."

MOUNTAINS CRUMBLE

Pohatu was the first of the Toa to reach his own village. Po-Koro was located in the barren, rocky desert. The Po-Matoran had built sturdy dwellings of rock and sand that blended in with the desert's craggy peaks and blowing dunes.

As he drew near Po-Koro, Pohatu realized that the land before him looked much different than the last time he'd come this way.

"Bohrok," he muttered grimly. The village was in danger — even from this distance, he could see the Bohrok swarms moving along the Path of Prophecies, closer and closer to the gates of Po-Koro.

Pohatu raced forward. "So we're playing host to the Pahrak, eh?" he murmured. "Well, I'm not feeling very welcoming right now."

He leaped over a fallen monument and looked around. Turaga Onewa was struggling against a Pahrak, trying to keep it from knocking over another monument. But the insectlike creature hardly seemed to notice the blows. It pushed past the Turaga and crashed against the tall carved stone.

"Stand aside, Onewa!" Pohatu cried, racing toward the Pahrak.

"Pohatu!" Onewa exclaimed with relief. "It is good to see you. Especially now."

Pohatu flashed a rueful grin. "It's good to feel so loved, my friend," he quipped. "Quick now — the monuments are already lost. We need to focus on protecting the village itself."

Onewa nodded. "I will alert the others. We will protect the village gates — whatever it takes." With that, he hurried off.

The Toa turned back to the Pahrak. They were everywhere — too many to count.

"Gather the krana," he reminded himself in a murmur. "That's the key. We need those krana."

Pohatu leaped onto the back of a nearby

Pahrak. He held on tightly as the Pahrak bucked and leaped, trying to dislodge him. Its moves were slow and easy to manage — until it marched toward one of the monuments, an intricately carved arching stone. The Pahrak ducked beneath, scraping the Toa off on the overhanging stone.

"Oof!" Pohatu cried as he hit the ground. "All right, so you want to play dirty, eh, Pahrak?"

The Pahrak took no notice of the Toa or his words. It was already trying to topple another monument. Dusting himself off, Pohatu raced past the creature. He stood on the other side of the Rahi Stone and leaned against it. The great stone trembled against his hands as the Pahrak on the other side shoved at it.

Taking a deep breath, the Toa of Stone stepped back and then leaped forward, aiming a powerful kick at the center of the stone. The great monument toppled forward immediately, and there was a shriek of surprise from the other side.

CRAAAASSSSSSSH — KRUK!

The enormous stone crashed to the ground —with the Pahrak trapped underneath.

"Sorry, my ugly friend," Pohatu said, stepping forward and wrenching the headplate off the creature. "I'm afraid you have something I need." He carefully lifted the glowing green krana from within. He was pleased to see that it was slightly different in shape from the one they'd found back in Ta-Koro. Good — that was one more toward the set of Pahrak krana they needed.

He tucked it into his belt and leaped back into action, heading for the next Pahrak.

Pohatu wasn't sure how much time had passed when he heard a shout from above.

"More are coming!"

He glanced up and saw that the shout had come from the lookout post atop the village gates, where a villager was scanning the horizon.

The Toa of Stone hooked his climbing claws into the gate and swung himself up to the lookout. Another swarm of Bohrok was heading toward the village. They were Lehvak, judging by their bright green color and the way they melted everything in their path by shooting acid out of their curved claws.

"What should we do?" the Matoran asked.

Pohatu's heart sank. Though he had been successful in gaining a few more krana, he'd been unable to drive off the Pahrak swarms. And now there would be more. . . .

But his voice was steady as he replied, "What else can we do, little brother, but let them come, and fight them when they get here?"

Then he leaped down to meet the Lehvak, ready to defend his village and his people.

EARTH TREMBLES

Onua was walking through a tunnel that led toward the village of Onu-Koro.

These Bohrok will stop at nothing until Mata Nui has been completely leveled, he mused. *But why?*

He paused, hearing a faint sound from somewhere off to the left.

CHINNGCH! CHINNGCH! CHINNGCH!

Onua frowned. That didn't sound like any digging or mining tool he knew.

"Bohrok," he murmured. "I wonder where you are? Let's see if we can find a shortcut."

He listened for another second or two, and then struck with his fists. He broke through the tunnel wall, burrowing straight through the solid earth. He burst through a moment later into a cavern that lay just a few hundred yards from the arched stone gates of Onu-Koro.

The place was crawling with the dark, smooth shapes of Bohrok. As Onua watched, a pair of the creatures drilled a series of short tunnels into the wall on the far side of the cave. The wall shuddered and shifted.

"Hey!" Onua cried. But it was too late. The wall and the ceiling above crumbled and fell in on itself, raining debris onto the ground. The Bohrok moved on to another spot a few yards away. The rest of the swarm were drilling in other spots along the wall — if Onua didn't stop them, they would bring down the entire cavern.

Nuhvok. That was what the Turaga had called them — swarms of Bohrok that tunneled deep underground, destroying the island from the inside out.

He leaped forward, grabbing the nearest Bohrok. It let out a hiss of annoyance and tossed him away.

Surprised at the creature's strength, Onua

resumed his attack. "Don't think you can get away with that."

This time he grabbed the creature by one of its legs, flipping it head over heels. The Nuhvok's headplate struck a rock and flipped open.

"That's more like it," Onua said, grabbing the glowing green krana inside and peeling it free.

He left the Nuhvok and moved on, glancing at the krana he held as he did. Its shape was slightly different from the one Tahu had removed outside Ta-Koro.

Over the next few minutes, he managed to gather several more krana. It wasn't an easy task — the Bohrok were strong, and whenever one came to another's aid Onua quickly found himself overpowered. Several times, only the Nuhvok's slow reactions saved the Toa from disaster.

"This is taking too long," he said. As long as there were so many of them, so totally focused on destruction that they couldn't be distracted . . .

Onua suddenly stood up straight. He had an idea — a way he might be able to use the

Bohrok's own focus against them. Glancing out of his tunnel, he noted that the Nuhvok were methodically taking down the dozen or so stone columns that helped support the cavern's roof. They seemed determined to destroy each column and collapse the entire cavern.

Dodging the slow-moving creatures, which ignored him as usual, Onua raced to the center of the room, where a cluster of columns still stood.

I just need a few seconds. . . .

He quickly dug a trench in the floor, a skinny moat surrounding the group of columns.

Then he waited.

It wasn't long before several Nuhvok turned their attention toward the remaining columns. One moved toward them, pausing on the lip of the trench in apparent confusion.

Onua leaped forward and gave the creature a shove. It let out a shriek of dismay as it toppled over, skidding straight into the trench.

"Now, let's just see if I calculated the width correctly," Onua murmured.

The Nuhvok fell about halfway to the bottom of the trench before the narrow walls stopped it. The creature struggled, its limbs waving helplessly. But it did no good. It was stuck between the walls of the trench!

"This is almost too easy," Onua said, stepping forward and yanking back the Nuhvok's headplate. He jumped back as the creature's clawed arm swung toward him, nearly connecting with his head. "Hey, I said *almost*," he added, ducking back in just long enough to grab the Nuhvok's krana.

Luckily the Nuhvok seemed to have more determination than brains. Several more fell for the same trick, and before long Onua had a full set of krana.

"There," he said. "That wasn't so —"

CHIIIIIIIIIIIIIIIIIIIYIYIYI!

A sudden scream echoed through the cavern. Onua spun around and saw a small Nuhvok Va careening toward him. He leaped aside, preparing to fight off its attack.

But the creature ignored him. It stopped in the middle of the cavern, still emitting its high-pitched screech. All the Nuhvok stopped what they were doing immediately and turned to face the Nuhvok Va. Then, as if with one mind, they all scattered in different directions. Within seconds, the cavern was empty except for Onua.

The Earth Toa stared after them in surprise. What had made them run away like that?

He hurried on until he reached the outskirts of Onu-Koro and gazed across the tunnel that encircled the village. The caverns he could see on the other side looked normal, and Onua let out a breath of relief, glad that his village had escaped the swarms.

"Whenua!" Onua shouted, calling for the Turaga as he raced into a spacious cavern. "Whenua, where are you?"

The Turaga appeared almost immediately. "Toa Onua!" he called out with a bow. "It is good to see you. The people are worried — we've heard terrible rumors —"

"What you've heard is most likely true. The Bohrok swarms have emerged, and they are on the move. I'm glad to see that Onu-Koro has so far been spared. And I intend to keep it that way if I can. I've just chased off a swarm of Nuhvok."

"If anyone can protect us, Toa Onua, it's you. Young Nuparu just left for the surface to see whether —"

"Shh." Onua hushed him in midsentence. What was that? He'd felt a vibration, a sort of rumbling. . . .

SWOOOOOOOOOOOOOSH!

With a blast of sound and fury, a raging tidal wave roared into the cavern from the next tunnel, sweeping away villagers, stones, and earth.

Onua was blown off his feet by the force of the first wave. It smashed him against the rock dwellings behind him, and he scrabbled for a handhold as he felt the wild current yanking him away again.

Must — hold — on . . . he thought grimly as his hands slid across a smooth surface. He couldn't see a thing — the water had knocked his mask askew, blocking his vision. But just as he felt his body being swept backward, the Earth Toa's hands found a stone bar. Whatever it was, he gripped it tightly, praying that it was strong enough to withstand the rushing water.

After several endless seconds, the water receded as the flood thundered on into deeper tunnels. Onua clambered up the cave wall for a better look at the damage. What he saw made his heart sink — the water hadn't had much effect on the basic structures, since they were carved out of the cave wall. But all the decorations and special touches the villagers had added to their dwellings had been swept away or destroyed. Lightposts had been knocked askew, their lightstones scattered. All sorts of debris floated on the water's surface.

Whenua looked out from the doorway where he'd clung through the flood. "We'd better find out if everyone's all right and get to the surface. It's not safe to be here — if another wave of water comes, it could fill this cavern to the ceiling."

Onua nodded. "Good plan. On the surface, we can seek out the other Toa and their villagers. The strength of these swarms are in their numbers — we need numbers on our side as well."

AMBUSH!

Lewa bounded toward Le-Koro, hoping that the Bohrok hadn't reached it yet. His villagers were courageous and capable, but Lewa knew that without him they would be no match for the Bohrok swarms.

Landing easily in the highest branches of a Madu tree, Lewa peered ahead. Smoke was drifting lazily up into the sky from the vicinity of the village.

Quickening his pace, the Toa of Air leaped from tree to tree, wondering how to protect the treetop village from attack. *Perhaps it's as Tahu often says — the best defense is a good offense,* Lewa told himself. *I could gather some of the village's best windriders and do a little cloudsneaking to find the enemy before it finds us.*

A stray breeze wound its way through the trees as Lewa neared the village. Tipping his face up to feel it, he launched himself through the air, catching the breeze and allowing it to guide him softly to the ground.

He landed by a gnarled old tree at the edge of a clearing. As he straightened up, he was startled to see that the clearing was filled with Le-Matoran. Turaga Matau was standing at the head of the crowd. He was clutching his Kau Kau staff as usual. But — what was that on his face, in place of his regular mask?

Lewa gasped in horror. It wasn't just Matau — all of the villagers wore glowing masks over their faces, each pulsing from a sickly green to a hideous orange. Behind the masked Matoran, plumes of acrid smoke traced ugly patterns in the air, blocking the view of the village above.

Matau smiled as he stepped forward toward the Toa, the expression grotesque behind the pulsing, unfamiliar mask.

"Greetings, Lewa," the Turaga said in a monotone voice. "We have been waiting for you."

DANGER BENEATH
THE WAVES

The route to Gali's village took her through Lewa's jungle-covered range. As she entered the moist shade beneath the tree canopy, she paused to listen. She heard only the normal sounds of dripping water and rustling wind.

Still, Gali sensed that something was not right in the jungle.

There are disturbances, she thought uncertainly. *Strange pulsations* . . .

Whatever it was, it was crashing through the underbrush, heading in her direction. A moment later she felt a blast of heat, and a dead tree trunk nearby burst into flames.

"Tahnok," Gali muttered sourly as more than a dozen red figures burst out of the woods.

She paused, watching as one of them breathed a column of flame at a lush Vuata Maca tree. The intense heat scorched parts of the trunk, but the dripping branches didn't catch fire. The Tahnok rammed the tree, but the Vuata Maca's deep roots held against the assault. Other members of the swarm were having similar problems.

"Not so easy for you here, eh, my Tahnok friends?" Gali said with sly amusement. "This place isn't suited for your brand of mischief."

The Tahnok Va at the head of the swarm paused, and for a moment Gali thought it meant to turn and attack her. Instead, it stood for a moment with its firestaff held aloft. Then it turned and scampered off toward the northwest.

"Going to visit Pohatu, are you?" Gali said. "Somehow I don't think he'll appreciate the social call. Maybe I can thin the numbers a little before you get there."

Grabbing a vine, she swung after the Tahnok. When she landed in front of them, they paused only momentarily before continuing on their way, clearly intending to bulldoze over her.

But the Water Toa was already gathering her energies, calling upon the elements to answer her. A moment later a rainstorm pelted down on the Tahnok, extinguishing their flame. The creatures gnashed their teeth furiously, darting beneath the trees for shelter. Soon the already swampy ground was puddled and soft.

The Tahnok at the head of the swarm scurried forward onto a particularly marshy spot. Gali held her breath, waiting to see if her plan would work. As the Tahnok took another step, she smiled as it began to sink, its powerful legs trapped by the sucking, wet soil.

The creature shrieked in annoyance, struggling to pull its leg free. As it did so, another leg got caught in the mire. Soon it was trapped, unable to move forward or backward. Every time it tried, it only sank deeper.

Now it would be easy for Gali to retrieve its krana. She wrapped a sturdy jungle vine around the Tahnok and lifted its headplate.

Soon she was holding the krana in her hand. It felt warm and alive, unlike the Tahnok itself, which had stopped struggling as soon as the Toa grabbed its krana.

"I see," she murmured thoughtfully, staring at the Tahnok. "The Bohrok themselves do not really live — they are merely vehicles for the true life force of the krana."

Gali wasted no more time. She raced for the coastline, anxious to see what was happening in her village. She resolved that once she had made sure her villagers were safe, she would return to the other Toa. Perhaps together they could figure out a way to stop the Bohrok invasion — before there was nothing left to protect.

LOST

Lewa tripped over a Bula root, almost falling to the ground. He growled in anger. Clutter. It was all clutter — these roots, these trees, the leaves and branches and stems and trunks. The water and the rocks. The soil, the sucking, spongy earth beneath everything else. All of it. It all had to go.

Clean it. The words echoed in his head, clear and strong and right. *Clean it all. It must be cleaned.*

"It must be cleaned," Lewa muttered.

He blinked, confused by the sound of his own voice. What had he just said? *It must be cleaned.* What did that mean? It didn't make sense.

It's a — a quest of some kind, he thought slowly. *A duty. But I thought — I thought I already*

40

*had a quest. A duty. Something I was supposed to —
supposed to —*

As his thoughts trailed off into bewilder-
ment, he was startled to notice that he now held
the tree root — the one that had tripped him —
in his hands. How had that happened? He glanced
down and saw the gouge in the earth where the
root had been ripped free.

Did I do that? he wondered uncertainly. *Why?*

Before he could come up with an answer,
he found himself raising his arms. A moment
later, a howling gale was whirling around him. The
wind tore the Bula tree straight out of the
ground and tossed it aside.

Clean it all, Lewa thought, moving on. *It must
be cleaned.*

FIRE AND ICE

Staring down at the krana throbbing within the Tahnok's bright red headplate, Kopaka fought off a shudder — not of cold, for the Toa of Ice never felt cold. Instead, he shuddered at the memory of what these creatures had done to his fiercely beautiful land.

After leaving the others, he had hurried to his village, Ko-Koro. Thanks to its hidden location beneath an enormous ice field, the Bohrok hadn't come upon it yet.

But when Kopaka explored the region further, he quickly realized he was too late. The Bohrok were already there. The Three Brothers Bridge, an ice bridge spanning a deep chasm between three glaciers, was melted into a puddle. Nearby, a valley once covered in blossoms of snow moss had been charred, leaving only a black hole in the ground to show where it had been.

One word had burned itself into Kopaka's mind — *Tahnok*.

Kopaka had trailed the Tahnok to the slopes of Mount Iho. He had battled the swarm with every bit of power he had, eventually managing to freeze one's fire shield into a block of ice while the others scattered in search of easier targets.

But it was only a matter of time before more Bohrok broke through to Ko-Koro and finished what they had started — melting away the village as if it had never been. Kopaka had been tempted to stay with his villagers and lead them into battle. But he had decided that if the other Toa had discovered any important information about the enemy, he should be sure to find out.

He had gone to Po-Wahi first, lingering there just long enough to lend some help to Pohatu, Gali, and Onua, who were fending off a swarm of Tahnok. Now he was going to see if Tahu was okay.

Who would have guessed I'd be rushing around checking on the others? he thought with a smile.

As he continued on his way, he spied a red creature in the distance — much like a Tahnok in appearance, but quite a bit smaller. It was one of the smaller, more nimble beasts known as the Bohrok Va, which acted as scouts and messengers.

Kopaka glanced around, expecting to see the rest of the swarm somewhere nearby. But there was no other sign of movement — just the solitary Tahnok Va climbing down the mountain toward the interior section of the island.

"Odd," Kopaka said to himself, watching the creature curiously. "I wonder where it's going all by itself?"

He skied down the slope, keeping the Tahnok Va in sight. The rendezvous with Tahu could wait — for now, it seemed more important to see where this creature was heading.

Soon the Tahnok Va had led Kopaka down through the foothills of Mount Iho into the area of cold, rocky plains lying between Ko-Wahi and

Le-Wahi. It continued on until it reached a flat, low-lying area littered with enormous boulders.

What is it doing? Kopaka wondered, staying out of sight behind a boulder.

CHKCHKCHKCHKCHK!

Kopaka spun around just in time to avoid a noxious stream of yellowish-green liquid. The stream hit a cluster of boulders instead, and within seconds the solid rocks had melted away into nothing but a bit of greenish steam.

Acid, Kopaka thought grimly. *So these are the Lehvak.*

The green-colored Bohrok were swarming toward him, destroying everything in their path with spurts of their deadly acid. Kopaka lifted his ice blade, preparing to defend himself.

But the swarms had no interest in him. They moved on to the east, straight toward the line of treetops visible in the distance.

They are bringing their blight to the lands of Toa Lewa, Kopaka thought. *I hope he is prepared to meet them.*

He turned to check on the progress of the little red creature he was following. But where was it? The Tahnok Va was nowhere to be seen.

Kopaka scanned the horizon, puzzled and annoyed. There was no way the creature could have moved out of sight so quickly — not in this mostly open area. Where had it gone?

He leaped onto the tallest boulder in the area, scanning the rock-strewn ground all around. He zeroed in on a cluster of especially large boulders, which formed a sort of ring — like a campfire circle for giants. There. It was the only place the Tahnok Va could be hiding.

Leaping easily to another large rock, Kopaka kept his gaze trained on the circle of boulders.

There, he thought, his head swiveling to focus on a flash of movement to the west. *What was that?*

He stopped and stared. The movement came again — a flash of sunlight against polished bronze. A small creature came into sight — a Pahrak Va.

The Pahrak Va trundled over the rocky ground, heading straight toward the circle of huge boulders. A moment later, it squeezed into a crevice between the two largest rocks and disappeared. Kopaka waited, but there was no further sign of the creature.

Kopaka knew that with every second, the Bohrok were destroying still more of Mata Nui. But he needed to know what these Bohrok Va were up to. So he waited. And waited. Unlike some of the more impulsive Toa, Kopaka understood very well that it didn't always pay to be in a hurry.

His patience paid off. Soon more Bohrok arrived and disappeared within the circle of rocks.

All right, Kopaka thought at last. *There must be at least half a dozen in that circle by now. I think it's time to see what they're doing in there.*

He stood and glanced toward the ground, judging the distance. Then he prepared to jump — but stopped in shock with one foot held in the air.

Bohrok! Dozens and dozens of them came pouring out of the rock circle, scattering in all directions.

Kopaka blinked, wondering if his eyes were playing tricks on him. But no — just below the boulder where he stood, a swarm of Tahnok passed so close that he could feel the heat rising from their shiny red bodies.

Of course. There had to be some sort of cave or tunnel in the center of those boulders. But a tunnel to where . . . ?

The stream of Bohrok stopped as suddenly as it had begun. Moments later, the creatures had disappeared, each swarm headed for a different region of Mata Nui.

Kopaka knew what he had to do. Leaping to the ground, he strode toward the rock circle.

When he reached it, he realized the boulders were even larger than they'd looked from a distance. Even the smallest rose many lengths above his head. Walking around the circle, Kopaka soon spotted an entrance burned straight through one of the rocks, large enough for several Bohrok to pass through side by side.

He stepped through himself, ice blade at the ready. But it fell to his side in shock when he saw it.

A tunnel.

Not just a tunnel, but an enormous, yawning chasm in the ground. It plunged straight down into the earth, neither narrowing nor sloping before its depths were lost in the darkness below.

And all around the walls, clambering up along steep channels carved in the stone, were more Bohrok. Dozens of them — no, hundreds. Ten times larger than any of the swarms he'd seen. Here and there a Bohrok Va scurried downward into the darkness, but the rest were moving in one direction only — upward, toward the surface. Toward the helpless lands of Mata Nui.

Kopaka gulped. This wasn't what he had expected to find. And it changed everything. . . .

He was tempted to climb down those rough, narrow trails to search for some answers — but no. There were too many of them for Kopaka alone. He needed to find the others.

He just hoped they weren't already too late.

THE BETRAYAL

Onua walked steadily through the rocky wastes near the southern border of Po-Wahi, wondering how the battle was going back in Po-Koro. After meeting up with Pohatu and Gali and helping them set a trap for a swarm of marauding Tahnok, he had left them to spring the trap themselves. Kopaka had already departed to check on Tahu, which left Lewa the only Toa unaccounted for. Onua had set out to find him.

I hope Lewa is okay, Onua thought with a flash of worry. *He can be so impulsive — acting without thinking, putting courage before caution. And these Bohrok swarms are really nothing for one Toa to tackle alone, no matter how bold and strong.*

That fact had become clearer with every passing hour. Everywhere he turned, Onua saw more of the Bohrok swarms — or the destruction they'd left behind. The creatures seemed willing to leave nothing untouched, from the trees to the rivers to the very land itself.

He hadn't admitted it to the others, but Onua was truly worried about the Air Toa. Lewa had been gone a long time — Onua was starting to wonder if it hadn't been foolish to separate in the first place.

Calling upon the power of his Kanohi mask for greater speed, he soon reached the region near Le-Koro. He slowed and looked around, noting the charred foliage and uprooted trees on all sides. He also noticed several steaming greenish puddles on the ground.

"Acid," he muttered, not liking what this might mean.

He stepped forward carefully, his senses on the alert. The last thing he wanted was to let the Bohrok take him by surprise.

Suddenly Onua stopped, seeing something glinting golden in the sunlight.

It was a Kanohi mask — Lewa's mask, lying

on the ground abandoned. He bent to pick it up, not liking what this might mean.

He walked on toward the outskirts of the treetop town. As he drew closer, Onua became aware of a sound somewhere ahead.

Onua took a cautious step forward, then another. *This jungle makes me nervous,* he thought. *All I have to do is find Lewa, and then I can get out of here.*

"I don't think it's going to be that easy," a cold, metallic voice spoke from directly behind him.

"Lewa!" Onua gasped — just as a mighty gust of wind sent him spinning backward onto the ground.

FRIEND AND FOE

"Surprise," Lewa sneered through the pulsing krana mask. "I heard you were looking for me. So here I am!"

Onua was speechless — it was Lewa, but this was not the Lewa he knew. The Air Toa wore a new mask now — a Bohrok's krana — and behind it, his eyes burned with anger.

"Don't try to fight me, Onua. You can't win. We're too strong."

Perhaps I should tunnel beneath him, Onua thought uncertainly. *If I can knock him off balance long enough to get my hands on that krana . . .*

"Just go ahead and try it, earthworm," Lewa said with a laugh. There was no hint of the real Lewa in the voice. "You'll find the ground here a bit marshier than in your wormholes down in Onu-Wahi. You'll find me a bit quicker than a worm, too."

"What — you — you read my thoughts, Lewa?" Onua stammered in surprise.

Krana Lewa chuckled. "I am a Bohrok Za, a squad leader," he said. "My telepathic powers are meant to communicate with my swarm. But your thoughts are so slow and transparent that I can read them with no effort at all."

Onua frowned. His chances were not looking good at the moment. The creature before him had not only the ruthlessness of the Bohrok, but also the strength and knowledge of Toa Lewa. It seemed an invincible combination.

But I have faced many invincible challenges before and prevailed, he reminded himself. *Perhaps if I approach things another way . . .*

"There is no other way," Lewa hissed, leaping forward.

There was no way Onua could dodge in time. He was flung backward and landed against a tree trunk with a thud. *When I went looking for*

Lewa, I didn't think success would be quite so painful, he thought, shaking his head to clear it.

When he stood, he saw Lewa watching him. Lewa's body twisted suddenly, as if fighting against itself. "Onua, get away from here — please!" Lewa blurted, the real Lewa. "Flee before I am forced to harm you."

"I think I have a better idea," Onua muttered.

He leaped forward, smashing the ground with his fists. A great wave of earth rose up like a tidal wave, sweeping toward Krana Lewa.

But the infected Toa somersaulted easily over the passing quake. "Leave while there's still time," Lewa cried, his voice filled with pain. "I can feel the power building! Even your strength won't be able to defeat me soon."

Onua wasn't sure what to try next. Lewa was strong in battle — too strong. He wasn't sure he could defeat him. But he certainly wasn't going to allow this — this krana thing to see that.

Or was he right in thinking of Lewa that

way? No matter what he might wear on his face, beneath the mask he was still Lewa — Toa, friend, hero.

"I know the krana controls your body," he told Lewa calmly, lowering his arms to his side. "But not your will. If it is so strong that it can make you harm a friend, then go ahead. I will not defend myself. But I know you, Lewa. And I know you are stronger than this — this parasite."

Reaching out, he clasped Lewa's hand in his own. He stared into his friend's eyes — looking past the sickly reddish glow of the krana mask, searching for the real Lewa beneath.

"You are a Toa," Onua finished simply. "Prove yourself worthy of the name."

And he waited to see what would happen.

13

THE NEST

Tahu was uncharacteristically silent as he and Kopaka climbed the foothills at the base of the volcano. Though he didn't like to admit it, the Fire Toa was a bit awed by what the Ice Toa had just showed him — a nest of Bohrok. Tahu had been ready to charge down into the tunnel immediately, but Kopaka had convinced him to wait. It was time to join forces with the other Toa.

I suppose he was right about that, Tahu thought with a grimace. *I hate it when he's right.*

How much time had passed since the Bohrok had first appeared? Tahu wasn't sure; he'd been too busy fighting them to keep track. All he knew was that there seemed to be endless numbers of swarms and that their attacks were taking a toll on Mata Nui.

They passed a jagged patch of ice jutting out of the rocks just ahead. Clearly, the Kohrak had been this way. Tahu waited until they had come even with the icy patch, then pointed his sword, blasting the ice into lava.

Kopaka shot him an unreadable glance. "We will be needing all of our power soon," he commented. "Waste it not."

Tahu scowled. "Waste?" he said. "The only thing wasted is your breath when you tell me what to do."

"Yes, it seems so," Kopaka replied icily. "The Toa of Fire listens to none but himself."

Tahu's scowl deepened. "Is that supposed to be an insult?" he said. "Because I —"

Before he could finish his retort, a shout came from just down the slope.

"Brother Tahu! Brother Kopaka! There you are!"

Tahu had never been so glad to hear Gali's voice. He spun around and peered down the slope. Two figures were hurrying toward them.

"Greetings, brothers!" Pohatu cried. "You'll

be happy to hear that at least one Tahnok swarm is no more. What news do you have on your end?"

Tahu clanked his fist against Pohatu's, then Gali's. "Serious news," he said. "Kopaka tracked one of the Bohrok Va back to its nest."

"Nest?" Gali repeated curiously. "But how can that be? Nests are for birds and reptiles and other living things, while the Bohrok don't really live. They're just —"

"— vehicles for the krana they carry within," Tahu finished for her with a nod. "Yes, we realize that now, too. But don't you see? The Bohrok and the krana emerged from this nest. That means —"

"— that they spring from Mata Nui itself." This time it was Pohatu who finished the sentence. "They are not invaders from elsewhere, but creatures of the island just as all the others are."

"Right." Gali looked at each of the other Toa in turn. "So why are they trying to destroy their own land?"

Nobody had an answer for that. Finally Tahu shrugged. "We don't need to understand them," he pointed out, impatience welling up in him like lava. "We just need to stop them. So what are we waiting for?"

"Onua and Lewa," Kopaka answered. "Where are they?"

"No one has seen Lewa since we parted in Ta-Koro," Pohatu said. "Onua went to look for him, but we haven't seen him since then."

Tahu was ready for action. "So let's send a search party, or —"

"No need for that, brother Tahu," a voice sang out from behind a large stone outcropping. A moment later Lewa sprang into sight. He hurried toward the others.

"Lewa!" Gali cried with relief. "Are you all right? You look a bit — er, strange."

"And no wonder," Onua's familiar voice rang out from just behind Lewa. "Wait until you hear about the trouble our high-flying brother here got himself into."

Tahu glanced at Lewa, expecting a quip or other playful comment, but the Toa of Air seemed uncharacteristically somber.

"Yes, I suppose you should all know," Lewa said. "In case — well, just in case anything should — should happen."

"What are you talking about, Lewa?" Gali asked with concern. "Did you have trouble with the Bohrok in Le-Wahi?"

"You could say that," Lewa said quietly. "Not only just me, either. Le-Koro — Le-Koro is no more." He bowed his head.

Tahu wasn't sure what to say. He was used to Lewa being the flighty one among them, the lighthearted one who never took anything seriously. Seeing him like this was unsettling, to say the least. "What happened?" he asked gruffly as the silence stretched uncomfortably.

"It was the Lehvak," Onua answered. "They captured the Le-Matoran and infected them by replacing their own masks with krana. And when Lewa found them like that . . . Well, perhaps you'd better tell the rest, brother Lewa."

Lewa looked uncomfortable. "I — they told me it was a physical entrapment only, that they needed the strength of a Toa to offmask the krana from their faces. I believed them. Why should I not? It is not in the nature of a Le-Matoran to falsespeak."

"Unless in the interest of a practical joke," Tahu murmured under his breath. When Lewa looked over at him, he cleared his throat. "Er, I mean, didn't you remember what the Turaga said? That the krana, when worn, could steal the mind — even the mind of a Toa?"

"I remember that now," Lewa admitted. "I didn't then. I was too quickminded to help. And so I leaped right into the helptask, and before I knew it, my Kanohi mask was quicksnatched from one side while from the other, someone slipped the krana over my face. By the time I caught on, it was too late. I was . . . one of them."

Tahu wasn't sure what to think. *How could that have happened?* he wondered uneasily. *How could ordinary Matoran — even a group of them, even with the cunning of a Bohrok guiding them — overpower a Toa?* He shook his head. *It would not have happened had it been me.*

He glanced around at the others. Gali and

Pohatu were exchanging a worried glance. Kopaka was staring at Lewa intently, as if trying to dissect him with his gaze.

Onua was the only one who seemed relaxed. "Don't look so fretful, my brothers and sister," he said. "In the end, brother Lewa overcame the krana's power on his own. I stood before him, allowing him to choose his own fate — and mine. And I was right. His will was strong enough to overcome the poison of the krana."

"Only because you offered your own mindstrength to go with my own," Lewa said quietly. "Without that, I might never have found a way to self-free."

"That's the way it usually happens, isn't it?" Gali pointed out. "Even when an enemy is too strong for one to face alone, together we can find a way to prevail."

"Yes," Kopaka said. "And our greatest test of this unity comes now — as we go down into the nest."

"Nest?" Onua repeated. "What nest? What are you talking about?"

The others quickly filled him in on what Kopaka had discovered. Onua nodded as he listened to Kopaka and Tahu's description.

"What about the krana?" he asked when they had finished. "Do we have all we need?"

The six Toa quickly produced the krana they all still carried. It didn't take long to determine that they'd collected more than enough.

"That one is the Krana Za," Lewa said, staring fixedly at one of the krana. "That's what I was — what was infecting me, I mean."

Gali glanced at him with concern. "Yes, it's what *infected* you," she said. "But never think that it is what you were. Never think that you *became* the Bohrok, because you didn't."

"Gali is right," Pohatu put in. "Lewa, whatever you've been through, it's time to forget about that and focus on what's ahead. We'll need all our wits about us — no distractions."

"Yes, all right," Tahu said impatiently, not liking to think too much about Lewa's "infection." It made him uneasy — as if something alien had suddenly come into their midst. "Now come on. Let's go down to that nest and see if we can figure out what we're supposed to do with these krana."

"How do we know we're supposed to take them underground, into the nest?" Gali wondered.

Tahu shrugged. "How do we know we're not?"

"But we still don't know anything about them," Onua added worriedly. "We don't even know why they want to destroy things, or why they chose this moment to emerge, or —"

"Makuta," Lewa interjected suddenly. "It was Makuta. He released the manyswarms when we tried to awaken Mata Nui. It was not yet the right time, the time he had planned — but he out-sent them early, hoping to stop us."

"What?" Pohatu stared at him. "How do you know that?"

Lewa shrugged. "I don't know how," he said simply. "I just know."

Tahu nodded, understanding suddenly. The infected mask — the krana — must have transferred some of the Bohrok's knowledge into Lewa's brain. But if such knowledge remained, what else might linger?

The others continued to discuss possible courses of action. Kopaka and Lewa kept mostly silent, but the other three traded possibility after possibility.

As he listened, Tahu could feel impatience bubbling up within him. "Come on!" he cried, interrupting Pohatu's suggestion to gather the Turaga together for a council to seek any further knowledge that might exist in the ancient legends. "We can stand around here all day while the Bohrok continue to destroy our island and endanger our people. Or we can take action!"

"Tahu is right," Lewa spoke up at last. "We should hurry-go to the swarmnest. It's the only way."

Though he was glad for the support, Tahu once again had to fight back a shudder of unease. Was this agreement really coming from Lewa, the impulsive one? Or was it coming from the mind of the swarm, luring them into a trap?

Onua glanced around the group. "Does anyone have any objection to Tahu's plan?"

There was a moment of silence. Gali and Kopaka traded a look, but both kept quiet.

"Then it's decided," Onua said. "We will challenge the Bohrok in their nest."

Tahu nodded. "The Bohrok cannot be allowed to endanger our people any longer."

"No," Lewa reminded them. "The Bohrok are not the true enemy. It is the krana we must defeat. They have a purpose, a mission — it's why they exist."

Pohatu shrugged. "Then they can tell us all about it — on their way off the island."

THE CHALLENGE

The six Toa wasted no time in traveling to the mouth of the nest. They climbed down its steep, rocky walls, avoiding the emerging Bohrok whenever possible and fighting them when not. Their progress was agonizingly slow, but eventually they left the glow of daylight behind and found themselves in a large, smooth tunnel leading deep into the earth.

The darkness swallowed them up. Occasionally a group of Bohrok hurried past. By pressing against the walls, the Toa managed to avoid attracting their attention. Though they hated the thought of more swarms emerging into Mata Nui, they knew their energy might be needed for whatever they found at the end of the tunnel.

Tahu found himself walking beside Onua.

Lewa and Kopaka were walking close together at the front of the group, with Pohatu and Gali trailing just behind them.

"Keep an eye on Lewa," Tahu murmured to his companion.

"Do you think he is still influenced by the swarm?" Onua asked, glancing forward.

"I don't know what to think. But nothing can be allowed to interfere with our mission."

Onua chuckled. "Lewa would say you sound like a Bohrok, my friend."

Tahu didn't bother to respond. Instead, he hurried forward to warn Pohatu not to let his guard down around Lewa.

A few minutes later, there was a scraping sound as Pohatu ran his hand along the tunnel wall. "Have you noticed?" he commented, loudly enough for all to hear. "This tunnel wall — it's smooth. No Matoran dug this. Or any Bohrok, for that matter."

"Are you sure?" Gali asked.

"Gali, if there's one thing I know about, it's stone," Pohatu reminded her. His voice held its usual light tone, but there was an undercurrent of worry. "I think something is very wrong here."

Gali didn't respond. *But whatever it is, we can handle it*, she thought. *At least, I hope we can.*

Just then Tahu shouted something from the front of the group. "What was that?" Gali asked Pohatu.

"An opening," the Toa of Stone replied. "Tahu is going down to investigate."

Gali nodded, watching as the Toa of Fire leaped off the edge of an opening in the floor. Moving forward with the others, she peered over the edge of the tunnel.

KA-BLAMMMMM!

Suddenly a stone door slid over the opening and slammed shut, blocking Tahu from view.

"Tahu!" Onua cried. "He's trapped down there!"

Pohatu's expression was grim. "And we may be trapped up here."

The Toa spent the next moment or two trying to smash their way through the wall. But it refused to give, even after Onua's pounding and Pohatu's most devastating kicks.

Left behind without Tahu's sword, the rest of them should have been standing in darkness. Kopaka was the first to notice that there was a reddish glow still lighting the tunnel. He pointed.

"Molten lava!" he shouted.

Spinning around, Gali saw that the Ice Toa was right. An enormous fireball was bearing down on them, filling the tunnel with its roaring, deadly energy. She desperately began pulling in water from the air around her, knowing that it was probably already too late. The only one who might be able to stop the lava now was —

"Stay back!" Kopaka yelled. "My ice can hold the lava at bay for a few moments."

He aimed his sword of ice, freezing the lava solid. Gali breathed out a sigh of relief, though she knew Kopaka was right — his defense would hold only a few minutes.

Pohatu and Onua were still trying to break through the wall separating them from the armor. They pounded against the wall with power that could level a mountain. Still the wall stood, not even a scratch marring its smooth surface.

"It doesn't shatter," Lewa shouted suddenly. "Doesn't shatter because it isn't there!"

"What?" Pohatu gasped breathlessly.

Lewa waved his arms, a hint of his old exuberance breaking through. "There's nothing you and Onua can't bring down," he exclaimed. "So if this wall is still standing, it can't be real! Stop believing in it — and it disappears!"

With that, he stuck one arm straight through the solid wall. Pohatu blinked, hardly believing his eyes. How could this be? He struck at the wall, feeling the impact shake his whole body as his fist bounced off the impenetrable surface. Then he looked again at Lewa, who had disappeared halfway through the "wall" by this time.

It couldn't be — and yet it was. The wall was nothing but an illusion! *What kind of creatures are we dealing with here, anyway?* Pohatu wondered, a shiver of dread coursing through him.

Noticing that the other four Toa had disappeared through the wall, Pohatu took a deep breath. If they could do it, he could do it, too.

Stand aside, wall, he thought with a rueful smile. *If I can't get through you with my fists and feet, I suppose this way will do.*

Trusting his comrades' wisdom, he flung himself at the wall. This time, instead of bouncing off, he stumbled right through.

He found himself standing with the others in a small chamber lit by a strange greenish glow.

"What about Tahu?" Onua said. "We can't leave him back there."

The others agreed. But before they could figure out what to do, Lewa pointed out that the ground was getting hot. Was it more lava? Or —

"Everyone down," Kopaka barked. "NOW!"

Kopaka rarely gave an order, but there was no disregarding his urgent tone this time. They all flung themselves to the floor — just as the cavern exploded around them.

Dirt, stone, and lava flew in every direction. In the midst of it was a tall red figure.

"Tahu!" Lewa cried. "Are you all right?"

Tahu nodded. Then, a little breathless, he explained that he'd used his sword to heat the air in the cavern where he'd been trapped — the heart of the Bohrok nest itself. The air pressure had finally blown apart the nest, scattering the remaining Bohrok to the far corners of the tunnels.

Before the others could figure out what that might mean, they felt the ground giving way beneath them. The cavern floor groaned and split.

"Uh-oh," Pohatu cried. "Looks like things are going downhill again."

He tried to hold on to the walls, but the entire floor was falling away beneath his feet. He skidded through the yawning opening. All around him, he could see the other Toa falling as well.

"Use your levitation powers!" Gali shouted.

"And be ready for anything when we hit the bottom," Tahu added grimly.

Each Toa called upon the levitation powers of his or her Kanohi mask, and they floated downward among the hail of falling stones and earth. The six of them finally landed in a massive, dimly lit, round chamber.

Kopaka found some deep niches carved in the otherwise smooth floor. Their shapes matched the krana they carried.

"I think this is where the krana are meant to go," he said, placing one of the krana he carried into the proper slot.

The others followed suit. As Gali fitted the last of the krana into place, there was a sudden jerk in the floor below her.

"Whoa!" she cried, grabbing onto Kopaka's arm to keep from being thrown to the ground. "What was that?"

More violent tremors followed. The floor, walls, and ceiling of the cavern shuddered.

"It's begun!" Lewa cried, barely keeping his feet as the earth shook and shuddered beneath him. "The end of the Bohrok!"

"What do you mean, brother?" Gali shouted.

"What do you know?" Tahu cried at the same time.

Before they could get any answers, the cavern walls groaned and fell away, revealing six enormous metal doors in the new wall. The doors slid back with a clang. Behind them were six identical tunnels shrouded in smoke and darkness.

Onua stared into the nearest doorway. "It seems," he said slowly, "we've been invited in."

THE BOHROK QUEENS

Each of the Toa stepped into the closest tunnel. Ahead, Lewa saw a dark glow. It held a strange shape—some kind of armor. Could it be?

He hurried forward and saw that he'd been right — it was a suit of armor! Exo-Toa armor. He didn't know how he knew it was called that, he just knew. More knowledge left over from the krana that had infected him? Shrugging off the disturbing thought, he took a step closer to the armor.

I suppose I'd better put it on, he thought, touching the smooth surface of the armor. *I may need it.*

Soon he was outfitted in the armor. He felt new power seeping into his limbs and smiled. Then his smile faded as he felt a tug on the edges of his mind.

Clean it all. It must be cleaned.

"No!" he muttered aloud, shaking off the shadowy thoughts.

Hurrying forward, his new armor clanking softly as he moved, Lewa wondered what he would find at the end of the tunnel.

All obstacles must be removed.

Lewa hesitated. Had that thought come from his mind? Was it the remains of the Bohrok's infection?

"No," he muttered uncertainly. "It wasn't — I didn't . . ."

You are an obstacle, the mind-voice came again. *You must be removed.*

Lewa gasped as an enormous creature burst into view, the massive bulk of its gleaming red limbs and pearly fangs filling the tunnel. "What — what are you?" the Toa cried in surprise.

This time knowing laughter filled his mind. *You know who I am, Toa of the Bohrok,* the voice taunted. *You know me — I am your queen. My sister, Cahdok, and I rule your thoughts, your actions.*

"No!" Lewa shouted furiously. "I *do* know

who you are, Gahdok." The name had popped into his mind as if planted there. "But you are sorrywrong about me. You don't rule me, and you never will!"

With that, he lashed out furiously. But the creature before him knocked him aside easily, sending him spinning into the hard tunnel wall.

You are wrong about that, Toa of Nothing, the mind-voice hissed. *Dead wrong.*

More voices started to whisper within Lewa's head — the voices of the swarm, calling him to fulfill their destiny. Gritting his teeth, Lewa did his best to ignore them.

I have to fight back, he told himself. *I am a Toa.*

He raised his arms, focusing his powers on the air around him. But all that came to him was a whisper of a breeze.

What's happening? Lewa wondered desperately as the voices gained in volume. *What's badwrong with me?*

He fell to his knees, pressing his hands against his ears. Still the voices filled his mind.

Cleanitallitmustbecleanedallobstacleswillbere-
movedyouareanobstacleremoveyourselfcleanitall-
cleanitallcleanitall . . .

"Help!" Lewa cried. "Someone, over here! Quickly — please!"

Kopaka rushed to his side. Lewa was dimly aware that the Ice Toa was dressed in Exo-Toa armor of his own.

"Drive it back to the cavern," Kopaka said tersely. "We can't fight it here."

Lewa breathed out in relief. Miraculously, Kopaka's cool, no-nonsense voice had sent the voices away. Nearby, Gahdok roared in fury.

"Use the armor," Kopaka told Lewa. "Let its power work for you."

Lewa glanced down at himself, realizing he hadn't even bothered to examine his new powers. But he would make up for that now.

Noting the electro-rocket on one arm, he raised it and pointed it toward Gahdok. Beside him, Kopaka did the same. The creature gnashed her teeth and roared again, but she backed off a few steps, moving down the corridor in the direction of the cavern.

"She's awaymoving!" Lewa cried.

Kopaka nodded. "Go find the others," he said. "They should be ready."

Lewa didn't hesitate. He ducked past the creature. Careening down the passageway, he burst out into the cavern.

"It's coming!" he shouted. "Kopaka is driving the creature-queen this way."

Gali, Pohatu, and Onua were in the cavern. All of them wore Exo-Toa armor.

Pohatu glanced at Lewa. "Tahu has the other creature on the move, too," he reported. "When they're both in here, we can surround them and take them down."

"Good," Lewa murmured. "That will be the end of the Bohrok threat."

He wasn't sure how he knew that, but he knew it for sure. If they could only defeat Cahdok and Gahdok, the Bohrok would be finished.

Before he could tell the others, there was a

shout. Tahu had just driven a large, silvery-blue version of Gahdok into the chamber — her sister, Cahdok. A second later, Gahdok herself backed in from the tunnel, goaded by Kopaka.

"Drive them to the center of the chamber!" Onua called. "Surround them!"

But the two queens were already backing toward each other. Soon they were side by side in the center of the cavern.

"Strike now, Toa," Tahu roared. "For your villages and your people!"

Lewa leaped forward with the others, raising his rocket arm. He aimed and let it blast right at Cahdok and Gahdok. The other Toa did the same.

But the rocket blasts exploded helplessly several yards in front of the sisters. Cahdok and Gahdok screeched with triumph.

"What's wrong?" Onua asked, his voice filled with awe. "It's as if they're surrounded by some kind of force field!"

Suddenly Lewa knew the answer. It filled his mind, even as the queens of the swarm taunted the other Toa in their thought-speak.

Fools! Gahdok hissed in the Toa's minds. *By bringing us together, you increase our power! Now Mata Nui will be as it was in the Before-Time. All that does not belong will be removed — beginning with you!*

Lewa gasped in horror. Now that the sisters were together, their powers knew few limits.

Why didn't I know this would happen? Lewa thought in frustration. *I should have remembered — from before. I should have been able to warn the others.*

But it was too late for that now. The queens had suddenly gone on the offensive — Cahdok showered Kopaka with a hailstorm of stones, while Gahdok blasted Gali with smothering heat.

Did I betray the other Toa? Lewa wondered uneasily. *Did I lead them into this trap — could the Bohrok still be controlling me, even if I don't realize it?*

No. It hadn't been his idea to bring Gahdok to the cavern — Kopaka had been the one to suggest that. The thought filled Lewa with relief.

Don't feel too glad, Toa of Weakness, the sisters taunted Lewa in his mind. *For we have powers that will make your blood run cold. . . .*

"Nooo!" Lewa cried, but the words froze

in his throat as Gahdok turned her icy gaze on him, freezing him in place.

Meanwhile, the others were calling upon all of their powers to battle the sisters. Tahu blasted Gahdok with fire, but she retaliated with a barrage of hurtling stones.

"Tahu!" Lewa cried in horror, his half-frozen mouth barely forming the name. With an effort, Lewa turned his ice-encrusted eyes toward Onua and Pohatu, hoping they would come to Tahu's rescue. To his surprise, he saw that both were busy fighting — but neither appeared to have an opponent!

More of the sisters' illusions, Lewa thought desperately.

Just in time, the Toa of Fire used the power of the Mask of Shielding to block the stones. But Lewa could see that he was struggling to maintain the protective shield.

Nearby, Gali was fighting to stay upright as wave after wave of nauseating heat rolled over her. She didn't understand what was happening.

Somehow, her elemental power had deserted her — she couldn't even manage to call forth a trickle, let alone a flood, to fight the two queens. She could see that Tahu was having similar troubles — and the sisters were closing in on him.

"Onua! Pohatu!" Gali shouted. "You are fighting shadows! Tahu needs you!"

Luckily her words got through to Pohatu. *Shadows?* He stared at the hulking metallic monster before him. It reared up, preparing a devastating strike with its hooked claw.

"Forget it, brother shadow," Pohatu spat out, disgusted with himself for falling for the sisters' tricks.

He stood firm as the shadow creature struck. The claw passed right through him and disappeared in a whiff of smoke.

Pohatu whirled around, knocking Onua on the shoulder. "Brother!" he cried. "Leave that shadow alone — we have to help Tahu!"

Without waiting for an answer, he rushed forward and flung the largest rock he could find toward the queens. But they deflected it easily, tossing it aside. Pohatu growled in frustration, looking around for another boulder.

"All of you!" Tahu shouted suddenly. "Shed your armor! It hinders our elemental powers — and they are our only hope!"

Of course! Pohatu ripped off the Exo-Toa armor. Though he immediately felt power seeping away, he also felt his own natural strength swell to replace it.

Tahu was still struggling against the queens.

It's no use, the Fire Toa thought desperately. *They're too strong! How can we hope to fight them?*

The knowing will come.

The words filled his mind. Suddenly he knew what to do.

"Toa!" Tahu shouted. "Surround them! We must combine our powers."

Lewa leaped forward with the others. But he couldn't help worrying — what if this was another trap? What if the queens had tricked them into attacking without the protection of their powerful armor? If the Toa perished, who would be left to protect their people?

"But — the danger," he cried as the others moved toward the hissing, screeching queens.

Gali glanced at him in surprise. "The safety of our people is worth any risk," she said. "If power is all these creatures understand, then we will show them power."

Tahu nodded tersely. "Let's go," he said. "Lewa, either join us or get out of the way."

Lewa stared at the Fire Toa, seeing a question in his eyes. Could Lewa give the right answer to that question? Did he know the right answer? Suddenly he was certain that he did.

"Yes," Lewa said at last. "You are true-right. It's worth the risk."

Tahu smiled at him for a second, looking relieved. For the first time since Lewa had been overtaken by the krana, there was no suspicion or doubt in the Fire Toa's eyes.

Then Lewa joined the others in forming a ring around Cahdok and Gahdok. He closed his eyes, summoning all the power he could find within himself. Just when he'd reached the bottom, he felt Gali's hand grasp his shoulder. A new wave of power swept through him.

A howling gale swept through the cavern, sweeping the sisters into a maelstrom.

Soon a driving rain hammered down on the queens.

Seconds later the rain froze to deadly hail.

A shower of stones pounded the enemy from every direction.

Waves of earth rose up around them.

Blasts of fire heated the stone and earth into steaming lava.

"Keep it up, brothers!" Gali shouted. "We're winning!"

Fools! Gahdok's words seared through the Toa's minds like poison. The queens were writhing in agony as the Toa's attack continued. *You think you have won — but you cannot imagine what you have unleashed!*

Then suddenly, the energy sizzling around the queens condensed into a gel-like substance.

Protodermis, thought Gali in confusion. The mysterious substance had been mined on Mata Nui for years, its origins unknown. And now it had formed a barrier around the queens, imprisoning them within!

Before she could understand the significance of this protodermis cage, Gali heard a deafening rumble of earth and stone. The cavern shuddered as stones rained down from above and the earth erupted below.

A NEW BEGINNING

"Looks like Cahdok and Gahdok had one more surprise for us!" Onua shouted as he tried to stay upright.

Lewa shook his head. "This is not their doing," he called back, the knowledge strong in his mind. "This comes from the heart of Mata Nui."

"The floor!" Gali cried. "We're sinking!"

Before anyone could respond, the ground fell away beneath them. Tahu found himself sliding down a long, narrow tube. Its walls were clear, allowing him to see the other Toa trapped within similar tubes.

What now? the Fire Toa thought rather desperately. *Just when we think we've finally won —*

Just then the tube ended abruptly. Tahu found himself flying through the air for a split second, and then —

SPLASSSSSH — ZZZZZZT!

He was enveloped in a gel-like substance halfway between liquid and solid. The gel cushioned him, seeping into every joint, making him feel warm and cold by turns.

Protodermis, Tahu thought fuzzily. The substance seemed to be seeping into his mind as well as his body, making it difficult to think or move. *We're swimming in protodermis.*

The mysterious substance had been mined on Mata Nui for years, used as a source of power. What effect would it have on the Toa?

The Toa of Fire closed his eyes, feeling the protodermis surround him. He wanted to struggle, to fight his way to the surface. But he couldn't move.

An immense heat swept through his body, his blood boiling and white-hot flames flickering behind his eyelids. As soon as the heat had come it disappeared, replaced by an icy cold so deep that Tahu couldn't even shiver. Within a fraction of a second, he felt himself sinking into warm, welcoming water, deep and pure. Then the water evaporated away into a howling wind that swept him around and around — until he landed on the hard earth and felt himself sinking down, down, down into the stifling depths. Finally he hit the hard surface of a stone cliff, and behind his still-closed eyes it was as if he could see right through it until it held no mysteries.

Then the stone, too, fell away. For a long moment there was nothingness.

With a gasp, Tahu broke through the surface of the protodermis. Coughing and choking for breath, he looked around and saw the other Toa surfacing nearby.

They levitated up in a group, landing on a rocky ledge above the bubbling pit of protodermis. The cavern was empty. Cahdok and Gahdok had disappeared. But the Toa were even more shocked by the changes they saw in one another.

Each of them was still recognizable — but they had all changed. Instead of his golden Kanohi mask, Tahu's face was now covered in a larger mask of gleaming red, while his body shimmered in metallic tones of silver and bronze. The others had undergone similar transformations.

"What has happened?" Gali voiced the question at last. "What have we become?"

"More than we were," Kopaka answered, his cool voice tinged with the warmth of amazement. "More than anyone has ever been."

Sure enough, Tahu could feel power surging through him. But he glanced upward with concern. "Let us worry about why it happened later," he said. "There are more important questions to answer now. What happened to Cahdok and Gahdok? And how are we going to get out of here?"

The last question turned out to be the easiest to answer. Lewa's power of levitation carried them aloft, and soon they were bursting out of the darkness of the tunnels onto the surface. They flew high up into the air until they could see the island from end to end. While there were enormous areas of bare earth, charred rock, and other damage, the Bohrok swarms were nowhere to be seen.

"We did it!" Gali cried as the Toa settled back toward the ground. "The threat of the swarms is ended! But at what price?"

Tahu couldn't help wondering the same thing as he glanced at Lewa. But he shook off the nagging distrust of the Air Toa's mind.

"Nothing has been lost," the Fire Toa said firmly. "The protodermis has given us the power to protect our people from any danger and to heal the land. Once we were Toa — but now we are far, far more." He raised his magma sword, reveling in the power surging through him. "Now and forevermore, we are — the Toa Nuva!"

The cheers of the other Toa Nuva rose into the air. Mata Nui had been injured — but soon it would heal. The Toa Nuva would see to that.

And they would see to it that Makuta never again troubled this beautiful island — if he even bothered to try. Was this the end of their battles against the darkness? Tahu wondered.

Not the end, Toa. The words hung in the air — not as if they'd been spoken, but as if they'd always existed, independent and alone. *This is only the beginning.*